Facts About Elephants

Written by Lynn Nicol

The elephant is one of the heaviest animals in the world.

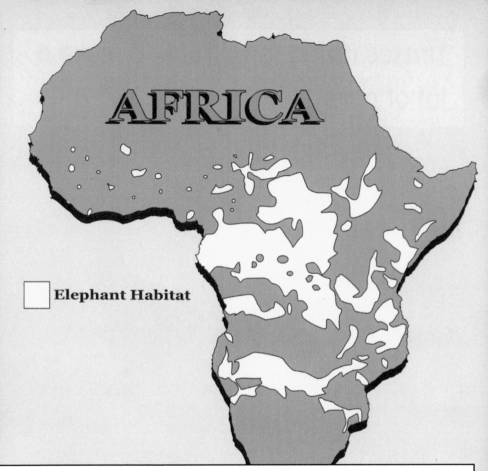

Elephant Habitat

Many elephants live in Africa. They are also found in some countries in Asia.

Elephants use their trunks
to call to each other. They make
a noise like a trumpet.

Elephants use their pointed tusks to dig in the ground.

Elephants like to keep cool.
They use their large ears like fans
to cool themselves off.

Elephants eat grass and leaves.
They use their sharp teeth
to grind up their food.

Elephants take care of their young.
They protect their small babies
with their large bodies.